Happy Holidays!
From
The 2nd Grade Team

Caitlyn and Craig the Crayfish

(A Lesson on Stream Life)

By

Michael T. Barbour

Illustrated by

Ashley J. White

8 October 2004
Revised 18 August 2005

Caitlyn and Craig the Crayfish

Published and Distributed by:

Rebel Publishing

436 Blackberry Lane

Myrtle Beach , SC 29579

Printed in U.S. A.

Dedication

For Caitlyn, whose curiosity is her window

to the world.

Acknowledgements

Thanks to Regina Scheiber and her help with the

digital images and the cover.

Caitlyn hurried from the house, anxious to begin her adventure.

"Be careful," her mother called. "And, stay out of the water."

"Okay," Caitlyn said. "I will." She skipped through the gate in her backyard and down the path to the stream that ran behind her neighbor's house.

Caitlyn picked her way through the tall weeds, careful not to step in puddles of water along the path.

When she came to the edge of the stream, she stopped and listened. The water gurgled as it flowed over the stones and passed her standing on its bank.

Caitlyn heard something else. "Don't step on me," came a small voice.

Caitlyn looked down and saw nothing at first. "Who are you?" she called.

"My name is Craig, and I am very small."

"Where are you?" Caitlyn searched the ground in front of her.

"I am here by your large foot. I am waving my claw."

Caitlyn then spied a crayfish on the ground waving its claws. She quickly stepped back. Then she frowned at the crayfish. "My foot is not big."

"It is to me," said Craig.

Caitlyn bent down to take a closer look at Craig. "What are you? Are you a crab?"

"No, I am not a crab," Craig said in disgust.

"Well, you look like a crab. You have claws like a crab."

"Umph. I am a crayfish. You can also call me a crawdad, but not a crab."

"Okay. So you are a crayfish. What makes you a crayfish and not a crab?" Caitlyn pointed her finger at

Craig, but not too close as she warily watched him waving his claws.

"There are many differences. I am long and narrow; crabs are fat and round. I can wave my tail; crabs can't. I live in freshwater like this stream; most crabs live in salt water like the ocean."

"Why aren't you in the water, then? Why are you standing on this bank talking to me. Hey, how come you talk?"

"Wait, one question at a time," Craig said, impatiently. "How come you can talk?"

Caitlyn thought about that a minute. "I don't know. I guess it's because Mommy and Daddy taught me."

"Well, my Mommy taught me, too." Craig thought about Caitlyn's other question. "Oh, yes, I'm here on the bank because my home is here."

"Where?" Caitlyn looked around for Craig's home.

"Right here behind me."

Caitlyn could only see a hole in the mud.

"This is my home." Craig walked over to the hole and pointed with his claw. "It's a great home. It is lined with nice wet mud and water is in the bottom. I have another entrance in the stream."

"Oooohh, mud. That doesn't sound like a nice home." Caitlyn wrinkled up her nose.

"Oh, but it is. It's a nice home for me. I like it."

Just then, they heard another small voice calling from the stream. "Help me. I'm stuck."

There on a stick in the middle of the stream was a little turtle.

Caitlyn asked, "Who are you?"

"I am Teddy. I got lost from my mother and now I'm stuck."

"What do you mean you're stuck, Teddy?" Craig asked. "You are just there on a stick. How can you be stuck?"

"I grabbed this stick as I was pulled along in the water current, and I climbed up on it. Now I am stuck."

"Quit saying that you're stuck. You're not. Just climb off and swim over here."

"I can't. If I get off this stick, the water current will carry me away. I am already far from home."

Caitlyn looked downstream and saw where the current slows down. "Teddy, if you let the current take you into the pool just over there, you can swim to shore."

Teddy looked to where Caitlyn was pointing. "How do you know the current isn't fast down there?"

"I can see that the water is moving faster where you are and that it is moving hardly at all just down there."

"She's right," Craig said. I know that pool and the current is not very fast. We will go down there and wait for you."

"I'm not so sure," Teddy said. "I don't know if I can do it. What if I drown?"

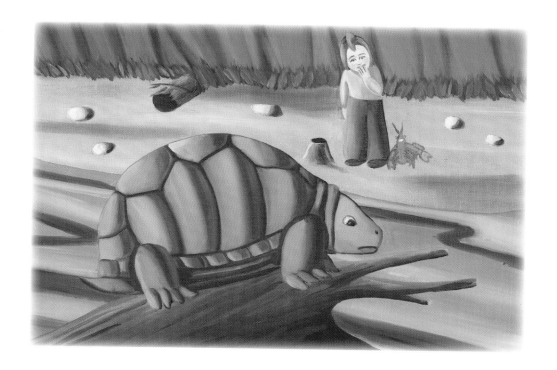

"You're not going to drown. You're a turtle." Craig laughed.

"Teddy, we will go down to help you once you get to the pool. Okay? You can do it."

Teddy thought about that. "Okay, but you two better be there."

"We will." Caitlyn and Craig started down the path along the stream to the pool. "Okay, we're ready," they called once they got to the pool.

Teddy took a deep breath and jumped in. The water current took him past the stones and past a fish watching him. He soon came to a quiet part of the stream. "This must be the pool," he thought.

Caitlyn clapped her hands and Craig waved his claws as they saw Teddy's head pop out of the water.

Teddy grinned (only as turtles can) when he saw the two on the bank. He swam over to them and climbed onto the bank with Caitlyn and Craig. "Thank you."

"You're welcome," Caitlyn said.

"I knew you could do it," Craig said.

"I don't think I could have done it without you."

Just then, Caitlyn heard her mother calling. "Caitlyn!"

"I'm coming, Mommy," Caitlyn called back. She turned to Craig and Teddy. "I have to go now."

"Will you come back to see us?" Craig and Teddy said in unison.

"Yes, that would be nice. I would like that. How will I find you?"

"Oh, we will be right here. Our home is here."

"Yes," Teddy said. "I think I like this pool. I will stay here and hope that my mother finds me. I will keep Craig company.

With that, Caitlyn waved to her new friends as she ran toward her mother.

The End

Novels by Michael T. Barbour

The Kenai Catastrophe -- Dr. Chad Gunnings goes to the Kenai Peninsula to investigate this wild corner of North America. When Chad and his associates are attacked at the Anchorage airport by members of the Warrior Society, a native para-military organization, they know that something very secretive is behind the problems in the Kenai. Their adventures take Chad and his colleagues to the site of a 100-year old massacre of an Indian village. What does this catastrophic event have to do with the present-day environmental problems in the Kenai? The surprising conclusion supports the contention that not everything is as it seems.

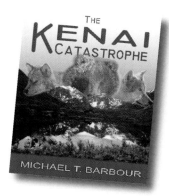

Blue Water, Blue Island -- The coral reefs around Hawaii are threatened by a secret enterprise attempting to tap into the extensive heat pockets of the earth's core. Dr. Chad Gunnings, an aquatic ecologist with the Phoenix Environmental Research Institute, teams with Dr. Kado Hashimoto, a marine biologist with the University of Hawaii, and Dr. Elice Morningside, an anthropologist from the University of Alaska, to investigate the accelerated bleaching of the coral. The three scientists face untold dangers from the denizens inhabiting the reefs, a fanatic determined to thwart any attempts to stop his illegal activities, and a mysterious woman with unprecedented skills in martial arts.

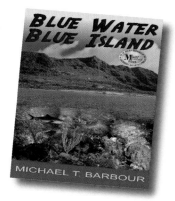

3929

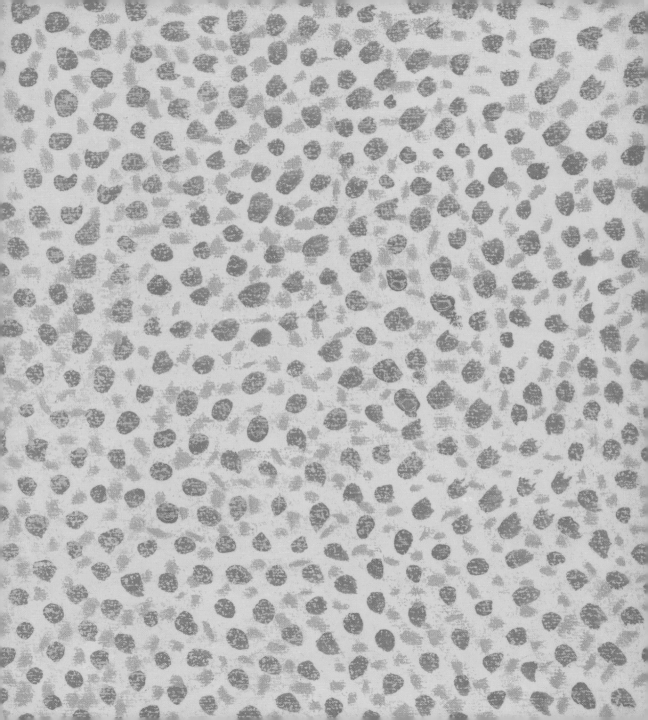

D.W., Go to Your Room!

Marc Brown

LITTLE, BROWN AND COMPANY

New York ❧ Boston

For my little sister, Kim

Little, Brown and Company

Hachette Book Group USA
237 Park Avenue, New York, NY 10017
Visit our Web site at www.lb-kids.com

First Paperback Edition: April 2001

Based on a teleplay by Kathy Waugh

D.W.™ is a trademark of Marc Brown.

Library of Congress Cataloging-in-Publication Data
Brown, Marc Tolon.
    D.W., go to your room! / Marc Brown. — 1st ed.
        p.   cm.
    Summary: When D.W. is sent to her room as punishment for
making baby Kate cry, it is Kate who finally makes her feel better.
    ISBN 0-316-10905-3 (hc) / ISBN 978-0-316-10670-2 (pb)
    [1. Sisters — Fiction. 2. Family life — Fiction. 3. Aardvarks —
Fiction.] I. Title.
PZ7.B81618Dwp 1999
[E] — dc21   98-42841
            HC: 10 9 8 7 6 5 4 3 2 1
            PB: 10 9 8 7 6 5 4

SC
Manufactured in China

It was cold and rainy outside. Inside, D.W. was playing with her blocks.
"This is *my* castle," she said.
"Glooba," said baby Kate.
"Don't touch!" shouted D.W. "This is *mine*."

Baby Kate took a block and laughed.
"Now look what you did!" yelled D.W.
"D.W.," warned Mother.
"She took my block," said D.W.

"Kate is a baby," said Mother, "and you're a big girl."
"I'm not a big girl," said D.W. "I'm a little girl."

Baby Kate took another block and giggled.
"That's it," said D.W., trying to whisper. "Give it back,
or I'll pinch you!"
When D.W. grabbed the block, baby Kate began to cry.

"Dora Winifred Read! Go to your room!"
ordered Mother.
"What did I do?" asked D.W.

In her room, D.W. stomped around. This is so unfair, she thought. I'm a prisoner in my own room!

"How will I survive?" she called downstairs. "I could starve."

"Dinner's in ten minutes," said Mother. "You can come out then."

D.W. looked at her clock.
It's not moving, she thought. It must be broken!

But when she went downstairs, Father wouldn't listen. "D.W., go to your room," he said.
"Okay, okay," said D.W. "You don't have to treat me like a criminal."

Back in her room, D.W. felt sorry for herself.
I'm just a little servant girl for Mom, Dad, and Arthur,
she thought. All I do is work, work, work.

Nobody loves me, thought D.W. And it's all Kate's fault!
Maybe we could sell Kate at the next yard sale.

Suddenly D.W. remembered that her new bike was out in the rain.

She ran downstairs and into the kitchen.
"The only bike I have in the whole world is outside in the rain!" she cried. "It's getting rusty!"

"I'll put it away," offered Arthur.
"Okay," said Mother. "D.W., go to your room."
"Will the punishment never end?" moaned D.W.

Grandma Thora is the only one who really loves me,
thought D.W. Wait until I tell her what they did to me.
She'll fix them.

Then D.W. got an idea.
I'll run away and go live on Button Island all by myself,
she thought. Then they'll be sorry.
D.W. was packing when Mother came in with baby Kate.
"Hi, sweetie," said Mother. "Would you watch Kate for a
minute?"

"First I'm punished," said D.W.
"Now I have to baby-sit the enemy!"
Kate giggled.

"Don't smile at me," said D.W. "This is all your fault."
Kate laughed and offered her pacifier to D.W.
D.W. looked at Kate.
I must be the meanest sister in the whole world, thought
D.W.

She gave Kate a hug.
Just then, Mother came in.
"Now, that's the D.W. I like to see," she said. "By
the way, your time-out is over. Dinner's ready."
"Dinner?" said D.W. "But we want to play awhile."

"Dinner's getting cold!" called Mother.
"We're playing dolls," called D.W. "Just five more minutes? Pleeeeeeease?"

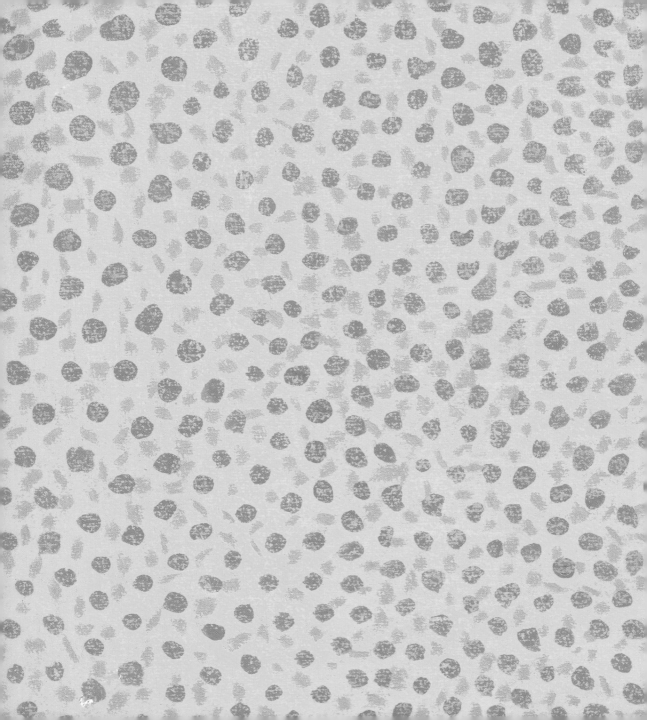

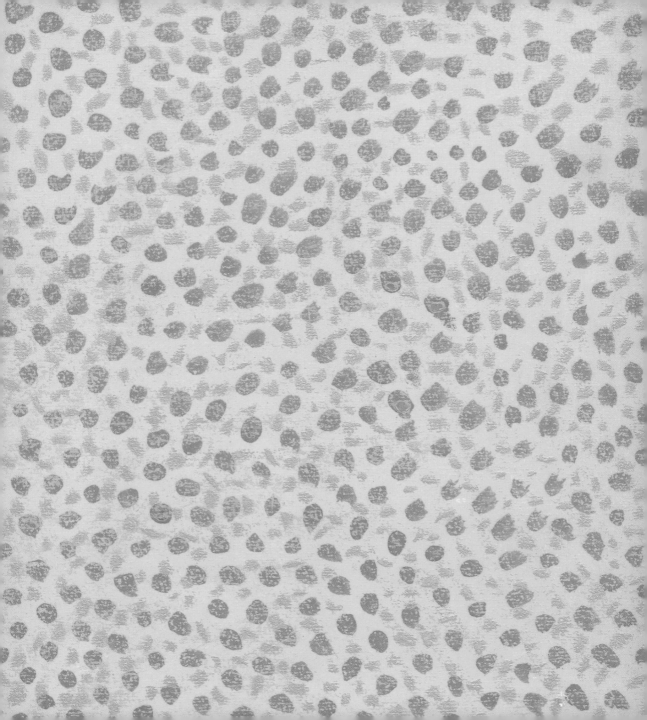

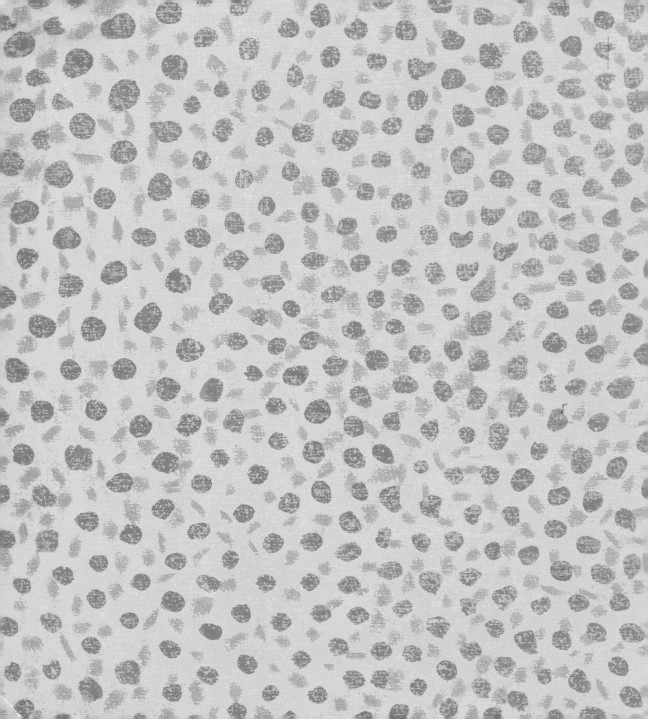